D1065267

The
Ancient Oak

Written by B.J. Jewett
Illustrated by Martin Bellmann

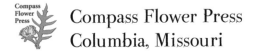

Compass Flower Press
Columbia, Missouri

Published by

Compass Flower Press
Columbia, Missouri

Library of Congress Control Number: 2023903908

ISBN: 978-1-951960-48-3

Dedication

This book is dedicated to Helena Clare Pittman, for her wisdom, guidance, and love in bringing this story to light.

And to all of you who understand the peace in standing beneath a big old tree.

Ancient Oak
stood with open arms
while forest became field
and field became houses,
until one day
it stood alone.

Each winter
the oak stood in silent greeting,
a hush of snow heavy
on its outstretched limbs.
Strong winds swayed
its sturdiest branches.

The old tree waited
for something it could not name.

With spring,
the oak whispered.
Flowers and leaf buds
burst to meet the day.

Raindrops fell softly
on a mother bird's wings
sheltering her nest
of blue eggs.

In summer,
the oak hummed.
Leaves sparkled by sunlight,
danced in the breeze.
Cool shade grew into a sanctuary
below its crown of green.

By fall,
Ancient Oak sang.
Squirrels scampered to
fill hollows with acorns.
Leaves turned
golden to red,
twirled by the wind
to settle below.

Ancient Oak had been here
watching forest and field,
sunrise and sunset,
moons crescent to full,
blue sky, storms, and the stars above
for as long as anyone could remember.

One day,
the tree saw a young girl
stepping softly through the tall grass,
drying her eyes.

She placed her hand
on its lowest limb.
"This is a welcoming branch," she said,
running her hands along the bark,
fitting her fingers into the
deep rippled grooves.

A welcoming branch.

Ancient Oak felt her leaning,
breathing in the sweet smells of
dirt and rain and earth.

"Oh," the girl whispered,
"you smell like home."

She began to tell the old tree
of her sorrows,
of moving here
from her home in the forest
to this house
at field's edge.

Ancient Oak listened.

The old tree wanted to tell her
it knew about loneliness,
of being alone in this field
where a forest of sycamores,
pines, and oaks once stood.

It couldn't.
But it could listen.

As the girl spoke,
a gentle wind
rustled clusters of leaves,
edges lit and golden.
A long legged spider
spun a web of silver.

Her words became softer
and her story drew to an end.

"Thank you tree, for listening,"
she whispered.

Ancient Oak watched her
run back into the sunlight,
turning once to wave
and brush the hair
from her face.

The next time she visited,
the girl stood below the twirl of limbs,
looking up into the vast crown of green.
"Hi again, tree," she said, climbing
onto the welcoming branch.

She pulled herself up
branch by branch.

She listened to the brushing
of leaf against leaf,
inching her way
along the scratchy bark.
"Just a little higher,"
she whispered to herself
before settling in the middle
of the old oak tree.

She heard a flutter,
saw a cardinal land nearby,
the orange in its redness,
its tufted crest,
and eyes that never stopped watching.

Startled by her presence
the bird flew away.

"Don't go," she called after it,
wanting one more look
into its dark, shiny eyes.

"I painted you in school last week,"
she told the tree.

"My teacher said you were beautiful."
The tree listened,
heard as she spoke.

She painted me.

The girl visited often.
As warmth gave way to chill,
grasses turned crunchy,
leaves curled at their edges.
The tree and the girl
knew autumn was beginning.

Each time she came,
the tree had an offering.
A bird's nest of tiny branches and moss,
acorns held in nubby shells,
clusters of lichens,
blue-green against
worn weathered bark.

One day,
she walked with a friend
into the shade of the old tree's crown,
stepping sunlight to dark,
through a pattern of dappled light.

The tree listened to their giggles.

At the welcoming branch
the girl said,
"Let me show you,"
and began to climb.
Together, the girls scampered
higher and higher.

They climbed
toward the squirrel's nest,
until they reached her favorite spot,
where they sat together
under a cloudless sky.

The girls laughed and talked
as the day wore along.
"Do you think the tree hears us?"

"I do," said the girl.

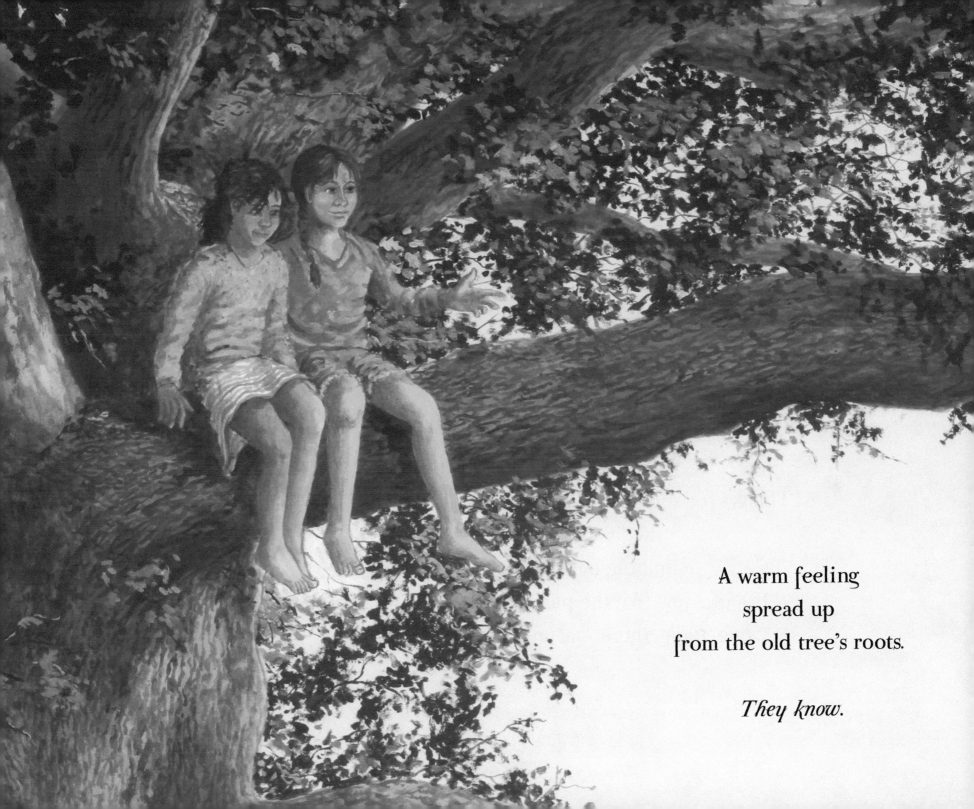

A warm feeling
spread up
from the old tree's roots.

They know.

"Thanks for showing me your favorite tree,"
the friend said,
climbing back down.
"It looks just like the picture you drew,
only today there was no red bird."

Ancient Oak watched
as they ran off together.
"We'll be back!" the girls called,
the sun dipping toward the horizon,
orange and pink filling the sky.

From then on,
each time she came to draw or read,
the old tree welcomed her.
If she sat by herself
to talk or whisper,
the old tree listened.

When she came to laugh with her friend
to climb high within its branches,
or sit, legs dangling,
the tree welcomed them.

Ancient Oak remembered
the day she first came to visit,
wiping her tears.

It knew her heart
wasn't heavy anymore.

The old oak
had been there waiting,
arms outstretched,
from sunrise to sunset,
moon crescent to full,
under blue skies and stormy,
beneath the twinkling stars
for as long as anyone could remember.

And now, it knew
what it had been waiting for.

About the Author

B.J. Jewett lives on the edge of a forest with her husband, three dogs, and two cats. As a child, B.J. spent hours within the branches of her favorite oak tree. Now her best days are spent with her daughter and grandchildren walking in the woods and searching the creek for treasures. Wherever she goes she is always on the lookout for special old trees, and enjoys photographing them as well as eagles and hummingbirds.

To learn more, please visit her website: www.bjjewett.com.

About the Illustrator

Martin Bellmann lives down the road from B.J. in a little log cabin that he built. In addition to painting, drawing, and photography he enjoys gardening and riding his horse.

For more information please visit his website:
www.blueheronmoonstudio.com.

Acknowledgments

A heartfelt thank you to my husband Bob, for his endless patience, love, and support. And to our daughter Megan, and grandchildren Lily and Nate, for bringing the best times into our lives. They fill our hearts.

A huge thank you to Martin Bellmann for painting extraordinary images that perfectly capture the essence of this story. He brought *The Ancient Oak* to life.

Much appreciation to Donna and Dwight Lenger, for allowing us the opportunity to visit and photograph their specimen oak tree. It lives just up the road from us, and I am fortunate to pass by it nearly every day. In all seasons, it is a sight to behold.

Thank you to Rose for serving as the model for several of the paintings of the girl.

A special thank you for Yolanda Ciolli, who was a pleasure to collaborate with on this project. Her expertise brought the book to fruition, and her patience and ideas were most appreciated.

CPSIA information can be obtained
at www.ICGtesting.com
Printed in the USA
LVHW070828110423
743880LV00026B/712